The Adventures of ARNIE the DOUGHNUT

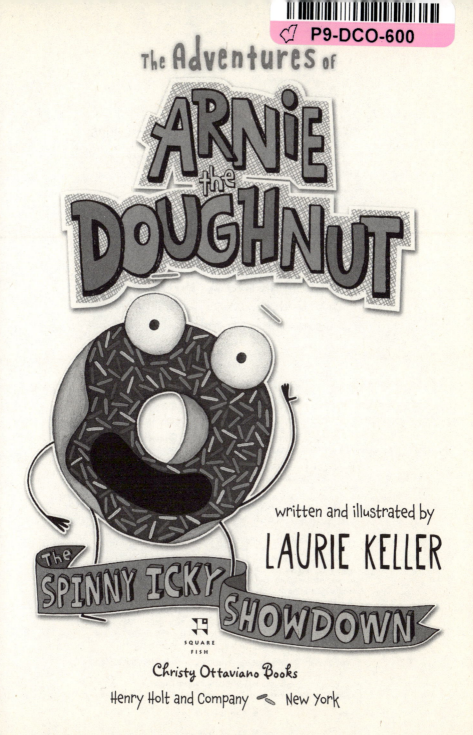

The SPINNY ICKY SHOWDOWN

written and illustrated by
LAURIE KELLER

SQUARE FISH

Christy Ottaviano Books

Henry Holt and Company ✎ New York

For my most favorite Otie-kins: Elena, Vincent, and Francis

Thank you to my clever friends and family for their "ICK games" inspiration and feedback: JoAnn Adinolfi, Brendan Callahan, Evan Callahan, Meg Cundiff, Galen Fott, Sarah Halliday, Charise Mericle Harper, Rob Hatem, Rilynne Locke, Scott Mack, Charlie McCarthy, Kerry Meyer, Carol Osborne, Christy Ottaviano, Deb Pilutti, Marilyn Quail, Jenny Whitehead, Pete Whitehead, and Amy Young.

SQUARE FISH

An imprint of Macmillan Publishing Group, LLC
175 Fifth Avenue
New York, NY 10010
mackids.com

Our books may be purchased in bulk for promotional, educational, or business use. Please contact your local bookseller or the Macmillan Corporate and Premium Sales Department at (800) 221-7945 ext. 5442 or by e-mail at MacmillanSpecialMarkets@macmillan.com.

Library of Congress Cataloging-in-Publication Data
Keller, Laurie.
Spinny icky showdown / written and illustrated by Laurie Keller.—
pages cm. — (The adventures of Arnie the Doughnut ; 3)
Summary: Arnie the talking doughnut and Peezo participate in a television game show, competing against other local teams in a series of challenges which include facing Nick "The Pumpernator" Pumpernickel, and still manage to solve a mystery.
ISBN 978-1-250-11499-0 (paperback)   ISBN 978-1-46687-031-4 (ebook)
[1. Doughnuts—Fiction. 2. Reality television programs—Fiction. 3. Competition (Psychology)—Fiction. 4. Mystery and detective stories. 5. Humorous stories.] I. Title.
PZ7.K281346Spi 2015
[Fic]—dc23   2014045707

Originally published in the United States by Christy Ottaviano Books/Henry Holt and Company
First Square Fish Edition: 2017
Square Fish logo designed by Filomena Tuosto
The illustrations for this book were created by using black felt-tip pens and Photoshop.

3 5 7 9 10 8 6 4

AR: 4.3 / LEXILE: 820L

2

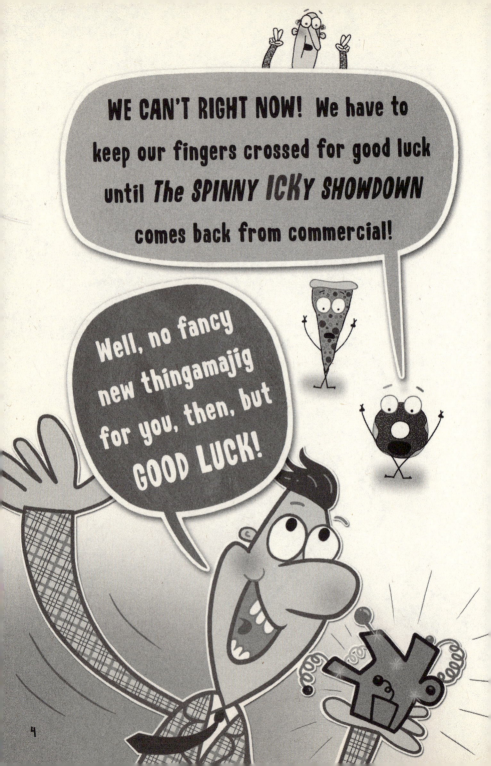

4

DARN, I would have liked a fancy new thing-amajig, but we CAN'T uncross our fingers because RICKy MaverICK, the host of *The SPINNY ICKy SHOWDOWN*, is about to announce the **one** and **only** town they're going to travel to for their season finale! *The SPINNY ICKy SHOWDOWN* is the BEST show on TV, and Peezo and I want to compete on it more than anything. Even Mr. Bing likes to watch it, which is saying a lot because he doesn't like the shows

DING DONG DOOFUS,
NOGGIN KNOCKERS,
OR
PLEASE STOP SNEEZING ON ME!

Peezo comes over every Friday night to watch *The SPINNY ICKy SHOWDOWN* with us. We laugh really hard through the whole show because the *ICKSTERS* (the contestants) have to do all sorts of crazy

iCK-related things

like painting a piCKet fence with lipstiCK or jumping like criCKets over candlestiCKs.

The *ICKSTERS* compete in teams of two and one team gets eliminated after each round. At the end of the competition both members of the winning *ICKS* team are presented with a **BIG, SHINY ICKS TROPHY** with their VERY OWN NAME engraved on it!

YOUR NAME HERE

When Peezo and I heard that *The SPINNY ICKy SHOWDOWN* was taking their show on the road, we sent in our entry forms RIGHT AWAY hoping they'd pick *YUMMY VALLEY* and choose us to be an *ICKSTER* team! We had to make up a team name so we chose

The DOUGH BROS

since we're both made of dough and we're SUCH GOOD FRIENDS we're almost like brothers, or BROS for short.

We're back, everyone, and it's the moment you've all been waiting for. We're ready to announce the one and only town we'll visit for the season finale of *The SPINNY **ICK**Y SHOWDOWN*! **DRUM ROLL, PLEASE.**

Eh-hem, I said, *DRUM ROLL PLEASE!*

That's **ODD**. Drum Roll Guy is **ALWAYS** right here whenever I call for a drum roll.

Does anyone know where he is?

Wait, are you sure he didn't say CRUMMY VALLEY?

By the way, if anyone thinks I said CRUMMY VALLEY, I didn't. I said YUMMY VALLEY.

All right, everyone in *Yummy Valley*, listen up. Here are the names of the five teams of ICKSTERS who will get their chance to take on *The* SPINNY ICKY SHOWDOWN!

The Law Lads
Officers Pete Pamby
and Dwayne Dwaggy

The Woolly Warriors
Carl Caveman
and Baa-Baa

The Curly-Cues
Identical Twins
Heeza and Leeza
Schmelly

The Grand Gals
Grandma Gloria and
Granddaughter Gabby

AND

Oh, please say the Dough Bros, PLEASE SAY THE *DOUGH BROS!*

Okay, I'll say it— the *Dough Bros,* Arnie the Doughnut and Peezo the Piece of Pizza!

LEAPIN' LONG JOHNS!

I can't believe that Peezo and I are actually going to **COMPETE** on *The SPINNY ICKy SHOWDOWN* and have a chance to win a big, shiny *ICKS* trophy! It sure would look nice up on Mr. Bing's shelf. Besides, I think Stiffy Stu McShiny up there would really like to have a buddy. Stiffy Stu McShiny is Mr. Bing's 1st place bowling trophy.

What do you say, Stiffy Stu—would you like to have a shiny new friend? You'll have to make some room up on that shelf because the *ICKS* trophy is even bigger than **YOU!**

1ST PLACE

CHAPTER 3

Peezo and I have to get down to business, as they say, if we're going to stand a chance of winning *The SPINNY ICKy SHOWDOWN!* We need to get as fast, limber, and strong as possible to be ready for whatever they make us do. But there's ANOTHER reason we need to get stronger—a LOT stronger— and it involves the one thing that Peezo is

MOST AFRAID OF IN THE WHOLE WIDE WORLD....

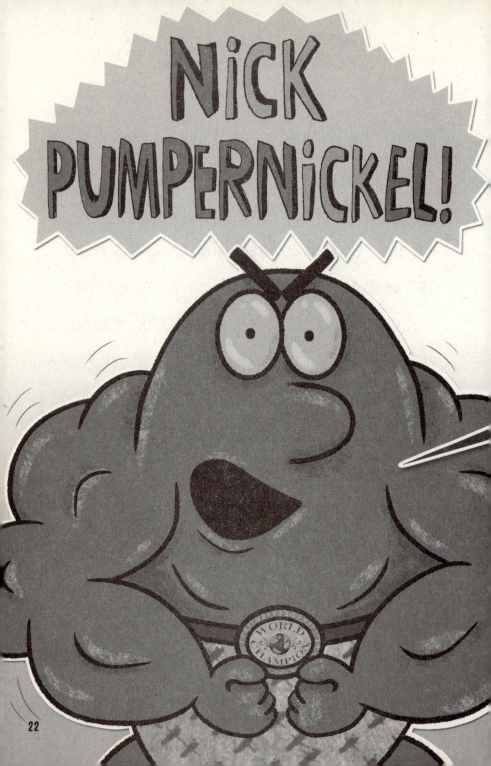

Nick Pumpernickel is a pumped-up loaf of pumpernickel bread and the most DREADED category on *The SPINNY ICKy SHOWDOWN!* He's the former *MR. WORLD WONDER LOAF* and calls himself the *PUMPERNATOR!*

HA! The *PUMPERNATOR'S* muscles are too pumped up to fit on one page!

Of all the categories on the wheel, Nick Pumpernickel is the one NOBODY wants to get because each *ICKSTER* team has to ARM WRESTLE HIM!

Nick Pumpernickel is **SO STRONG** that he even takes on both teammates at the same time—

one with his **RIGHT** arm

and one with his **LEFT**.

He taunts everyone by acting all **TOUGH** and saying rude things before they start, and it must work because **NO ONE** has **EVER** beaten him. If they **DID**, they'd get to jump all the way ahead to the final round. But since that's

NEVER happened, the way it works is, the team who lasts the **SHORTEST** amount of time against Nick Pumpernickel gets

DISQUALIFIED!

ELIMINATED!

KICKED OFF!

The teams who get to stay, though, are usually **SO TIRED** after arm wrestling him that it makes the rest of the competition even **HARDER** for them. The whole round is

TOTALLY HUMILIATING

for everyone. Well, for everyone except **NICK PUMPERNICKEL**, that is!

I don't care what anyone thinks—I'm not afraid of the *PUMPERNATOR*, and Peezo shouldn't be either. I know this sounds CUCKOO, but I really think we can **BEAT Nick** Pumpernickel if we start training right away!

Did someone say *BEATNIK*?

Oh, hi, Beatnik Bill. No, I said BEAT NICK. As in, I think Peezo and I can BEAT Nick Pumpernickel at arm wrestling.

Yeah, right. Well, good luck with THAT! Later, little doughy-dude!

I get the feeling he doesn't agree with me.

CHAPTER 4

There's a gym here at the apartment complex with lots of heavy weights to lift so we can get pumped up like that over-cooked bread-head, Nick Pumpernickel!

Come on, Peezo, it's time to pump some iron!

Okay, Peezo and I are all warmed up and ready to tone our **BUNS OF DOUGH!** We just heard the trainer lady tell that man to lift those barbells over his head **TEN** times. It must be working because even his **MUSCLES** have **MUSCLES!**

Three more!

All right, Peezo—you heard the lady. Let's lift these barbells over our heads ten times.

CHAPTER 5

ICK! ICK! ICK! ICK!

ICK! ICK!

Almost the ENTIRE town of YUMMY VALLEY is here waiting for The SPINNY ICKY SHOWDOWN bus to arrive!

Everyone is BUZZING about how surprising it is that the show is allowed to take place in this field. I mean, it's a perfectly fine field—even though it's loaded with HUGE CLUMPS of BUMPS, HUMPS, and LUMPS like most of our roads in YUMMY VALLEY. It's just that it happens to be right next door to the home of Maude Ellen Murky—better known as the

GRUMP on a STUMP!

She got her nickname because anytime anyone gets even CLOSE to her yard she climbs up on the big stump next to her house and yells,

GET OFF MY LAWN!

But apparently she's a big fan of the show and doesn't mind having the competition take place so close to her house. Well, hopefully that's true and she won't

BITE ANYONE'S HEAD OFF TODAY!

THERE IT IS!

THE *SPINNY ICKY SHOWDOWN* BUS IS FINALLY HERE!

I'm **RICKY MAVERICK**, the SPINNY, **ICK**Y host of *The SPINNY ICKY SHOWDOWN*! Please pardon my wrinkled suit, folks, but it was a **ROUGH RIDE** due to all the bumps, humps, and lumps on your roads! Our bus took **QUITE** a beating and two of my hairs actually popped out of place!

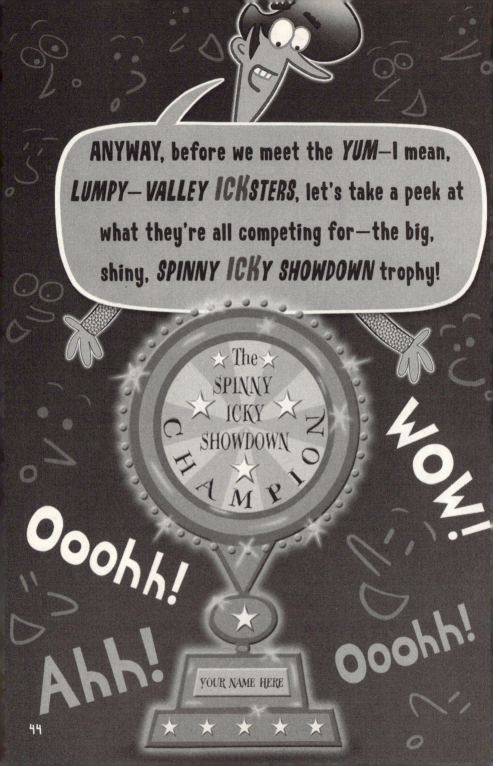

CHAPTER 6

All right, everyone—let's meet our *LUMPY VALLEY ICKSTERS*, shall we?

The Curly-Cues
Heeza and
Leeza Schmelly

The Woolly Warriors
Carl Caveman
and Baa-Baa

The Grand Gals
Grandma Gloria and
Granddaughter Gabby

You can call me BIG G!

You can call me LITTLE G!

WOW, Little G has the BEST HAT! It has a propeller-spinning penguin on top! Don't ask me why, but I've always had a fondness for propeller-spinning penguins.

Next we have

The LAW LADS

Officers Pete Pamby

and Dwayne Dwaggy.

Sadly, Dwayne Dwaggy dwopped—

I mean, *DROPPED*—out at the

last minute because of

an unfortunate hangnail

incident. SO, just moments

ago a NEW teammate was chosen from

the entries we received and that person is:

PIKYOR POCKETO!

Mr. Pocketo recently moved here from the little island of **KLEPTONIA**. Since Pikyor Pocketo isn't a police officer or **LAW LAD** like Pete Pamby, they thought it best to change their team name. And since both of their **FIRST** and **LAST** names start with **P**s they decided on

The **P. P. BOYS!**

Hmm, it doesn't sound as TOUGH when you say it out loud like that, does it?

And **LAST** but not *YEAST*—

Ba dum TSSSHH!

HA, a little baking joke there— we have the *DOUGH BROS*, Arnie the Doughnut and Peezo the Piece of Pizza.

I believe you boys are the first **FOOD** contestants we've had on the show.

51

And two last introductions before we get started:

FIRST, the *ICKY CHICKEN*! When a round is about to begin, she'll *BAWK* three times like this:

bawk bawk baGAAWWK!

That's your cue to get moving!

And FINALLY, the ONE you've been waiting for—the DOUGHIEST of the DOUGHY, the DENSEST of the DENSE, the YEASTIEST of the YEASTY, the *"PUMPERNATOR"* himself— NICK PUMPERNICKEL!

That's right, it's the *Pumperlicious Pumpernator*! Nick Pumpernickel knows you're shaking in your little baby socks, but the *Pumpernator*'s not afraid of you wimpy *ICKSTER* sissies!

It's okay, Peezo, don't let him scare you. He talks **TOUGH** but he's all **FLUFF**!

Hello, Peezo, I see Nick Pumpernickel has you ***ALL SHOOK UP***, so my sideburns and I wrote you a little song. I hope it helps.

It's "The KING"!

You're the shakiest pizza
That I ever met.
A pumped-up pumpernICKel loaf
Is makin' you sweat.
You'll kICK his molasses,
There's no need to fret.
Don't be sICK,
It's only NICK
PumpernICK-eL,
Yeah, yeah!
IT'S ONLY
NICK!

CHOPSTICK NICKEL PICK!

In this round you have to find the NICKELS we've hidden all over the large, lumpy bumps in the *Lumpy Valley* field.

That may sound easy but you won't be using your HANDS to pick them up. You'll be using a pair of SUPER DELUXE, EXTRA-LONG CHOPSTICKs from *Elaine's Super Deluxe Extra-Long Chopstick Emporium!*

OH—and you'll be wearing **KN**IC**K**ERS.

What are **KN**IC**K**ERS?

Well, there are **TWO** kinds.
ONE is a kind of men's baggy-kneed
trousers popular in the early 20th
century worn in such sports as golf,
baseball, and skiing to name a few.
And the **OTHER** kind is, ummm . . . errrr . . .
ladies' old-fashioned underpants.

Which kind will *WE* be wearing?

And here's the **KICKER**! Each team will **SHARE** a pair of **KNICKERS** (also known as ladies' old-fashioned underpants)—one *ICKSTER* in EACH leg! It might be **TRICKY** to run this way, but try and move **QUICKLY** because you only have three minutes to **PICK** the **NICKELS** and drop them in your **KNICKERS** (also known as ladies' old-fashioned underpants)!

The four teams with the most nickels will move to the next round, but the team with the least will have to leave with nothing but their few measly nickels and a single, unattractive pair of knickers (also known as ladies' old-fashioned underpants).

COOL! Peezo and I are **GREAT** at using chopsticks! Whenever Mr. Bing and his bowling pals order Chinese food, they let us play with their chopsticks after they finish eating. They're perfect for picking up and re-applying my sprinkles and Peezo's toppings after we get into one of our fake wrestling matches. But we've never used them while wearing ladies' old-fashioned underpants!

Also known as knickers!

All right, everyone, **TIME'S UP!** Please move to the judges' table and remove all the nickels from your knickers and drop them into the wicker baskets to be counted.

OH, NO! Our nickels are **GONE!**

Ours are gone too!

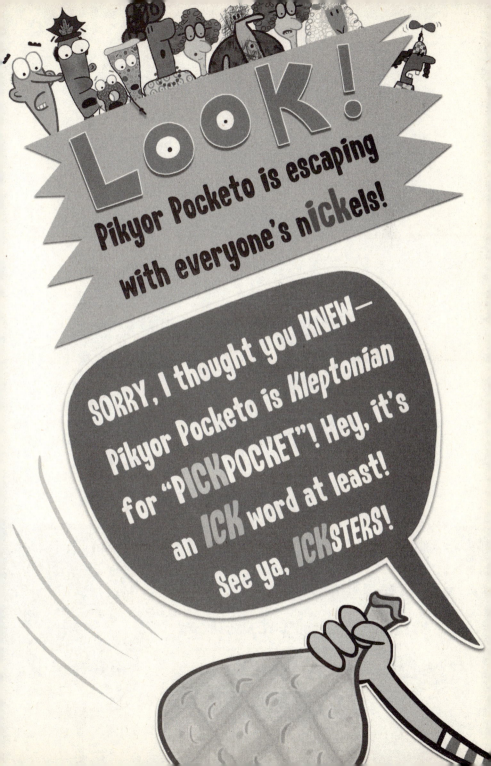

Don't worry, Mr. Maverick, Officer Dwaggy and I will get that PICKPOCKET!

But—my HANGNAIL!

67

Here, Mr. Mave**ick**, I can give you a chocolate-frosting do until you get your wig back—err, I mean, *TOUPEE.*

Frosting do's are all the rage in Paris.

A few sprinkles on top would look nice.

YES! Ricky Maverick just told us that since the P. P. Boys are gone, no one has to be eliminated and **ALL** remaining *ICK*STERS get to advance to ROUND TWO!

WOOHOO!!!

CHAPTER 8

I have to admit, I'm kind of relieved that Officer Pamby is gone. He always looks at me like he wants to buy me a ONE-WAY ticket to his stomach! At least now I can focus on the competition and have FUN. I sure wish Peezo could do the same. He's so worried about the possibility of having to face NICK PUMPERNICKEL that he's not acting like himself.

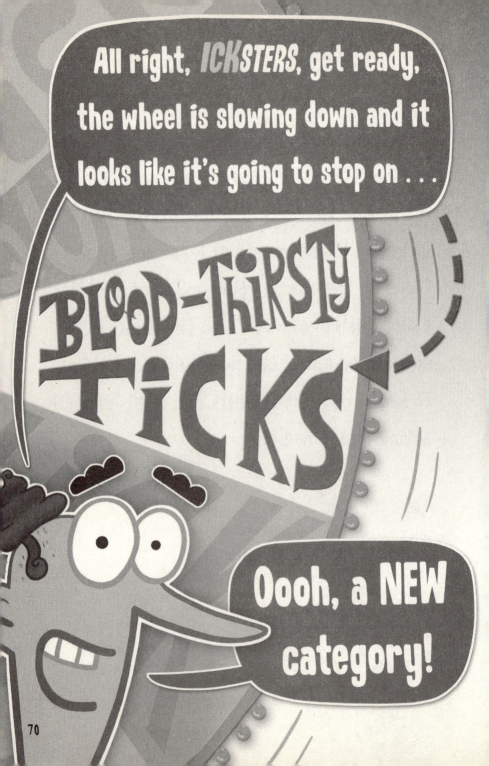

It says here that in this round, members of a hungry giant **TICK** family will latch on to and suck the blood of each *ICKSTER* until—

WHAT?

That's the most **DISGUSTING** thing I've ever heard! Who made up this category, anyway?

But it's EXACTLY the kind of thing I'M looking for in my new movie, *The Revenge of the GIANT TICKS*! Grab your filthy family, Mr. Tick— you're going to be BIG STARS!

Under no circumstances

shall the wheel be spun more than ONCE per round. Therefore, if ANY-THING should disrupt a round of play, such as blood-thirsty ticks, then by default the category for that round shall be *SEASICK VOMIT LICK*!

Spinny Icky Showdown Legal Mumbo Jumbo Book

Ewwww, that's even MORE DISGUSTING! Can we get the TICKS back?

GROSS!

Excuse me, **Mr. Maver**ick, I think we can help. Carl Caveman and I fell in love during ROUND ONE and he just asked me to be his bride!

Me love her.

We want to get married and go on our honeymoon right away, so there's no need to eliminate any *ICK*STERS in this round since we'll be leaving! Will you do the honors?

CHAPTER 9

After the newlyweds left, Leeza Schmelly
and Baa-Baa both needed new teammates,
and Leeza said Baa-Baa's curly fur makes him
the perfect CURLY-CUE, so we're ready to
go for ROUND THREE!

Ricky Maverick spun the wheel and it
just passed NICK PUMPERNICKEL!
Instead, it's going to land on . . .

YOU PICK
the
iCK!*

Okay, this is a **REALLY BiG** decision that could **MAKE** or **BREAK** our chances of winning. I've watched **EVERY** episode of *The SPINNY ICKy SHOWDOWN* and the *ICKSTER* team that gets to *PICK the ICK* always chooses something that they think they'll be **GOOD** at.

There's **ANOTHER** option, though, that nobody **EVER** uses, and I think it could really help Peezo—and all of us for that matter. The only problem is that I know Peezo would **NEVER** agree to it!

DOUGH BROS, I need your *YOU PICK THE ICK* category, please.

I don't care which category, Arnie, as long as it's not—

NICK PUMPERNICKEL!

NICK PUMPERNICKEL IS OUR CHOICE FOR *YOU PICK THE ICK*!

WHAT?!

I feel AWFUL springing that on Peezo the way I did, but I HAD to do it. If I hadn't, there would still be a chance we'd have to arm wrestle NICK PUMPERNICKEL in the next round and I just couldn't do that to Peezo. But with THIS strategy there's a MYSTERY ICK category under the YOU PICK THE ICK slot on the wheel that's only used if someone actually CHOOSES NICK PUMPERNICKEL for the YOU PICK THE ICK challenge. And whatever it is, NICK PUMPERNICKEL has to do it even if he's no good at it.

Little baby doughnut— the PUMPERNATOR is good at EVERYTHING!

But the **BEST THING** is that Peezo wouldn't have to worry about him **ANY-MORE**. Once everyone has challenged the **PUMPERNATOR** on the *YOU PICK THE ICK* round, his **NICK PUMPERNICKEL** category would be **REMOVED** from the wheel and replaced with a new category.

VOILÀ!

NO MORE NICK PUMPERNICKEL!

Pardonnez-moi, but *VOILÀ* is a French word pronounced *vwah-LA*. It means, "there you go" or, how you say,

NICK PUMPERNICKEL is good at FRENCH too! VOILÀ! HA!

All right, everyone, are you ready to see the category for the *YOU PICK THE ICK* challenge?

The Pumpernator will take you **ALL** down whatever the sissy category is!

HA! HA!

CHAPTER 10

Here we go, *ICKSTERS*! The never-before-seen category under the *YOU PICK THE ICK* slot IS . . .

It's a little RUSTY!

GRUNT!

CREEeak!

Errrr!

Got it!

PESKY PICKLE POGO STICK

Okay, ICKSTERS, with PESKY PICKLE POGO STICK you'll be POGO-ing with your plucky partner through PICKLE PASS, trying not to get pushed over by the PERILOUS PIVOTING PEPPERED PICKLES or pummeled by the POWERFUL PEEWEE PICKLE PUNTER or plunged into a PESKY PICKLE JUICE PUDDLE! WOW, that was a lot of Ps!

That reminds me. I need to

You'll have to hold it, dear.

NOW, if NICK PUMPERNICKEL beats all the *ICKSTER* teams like he does at arm wrestling, then the team with the slowest race time will be eliminated.

If there's a TIE, we'll do a tie-breaker. BUT if by some MIRACLE any or ALL of you BEAT NICK PUMPERNICKEL, then you'll automatically go to the final round!

Take your pogo places, *ICKSTERS*!

91

CHAPTER 11

Well, it looks like my strategy PAID OFF! Peezo is **SO HAPPY** now that he doesn't have to worry about NICK PUMP-ERNICKEL anymore! **FINALLY**, we can just have **FUN** and focus on winning the competition. GO, *DOUGH BROS!*

CONGRATS AGAIN, *ICK*STERS, ON BEATING N**ICK** PUMPERN**ICK**EL!

There's **ONE** last challenge and here it is: RICKETY TOOTHPICK TIGHTROPE! For the final round of *THE SPINNY ICKY SHOWDOWN* you'll each be crossing a tightrope made only of toothpicks!

A tightrope made only of **toothpicks?** That sounds **tricky!**

gulp

YES, and it's even TR**ICK**IER **Kicking** your way across! To find our champions we'll combine both teammates' crossing times and **KICKS** together. The team with the fastest times and most **KICKS** will be the *SPINNY ICKY SHOWDOWN* **CHAMPIONS!**

But what if we fall off?

GOOD QUESTION, LITTLE *ICK*STER!

If you fall off, don't worry—
you'll land in the soft pool of

ICKY-STICKY-THICKY GOO!

Try to make it over to the tightrope
ladder and get back in the race, but the

ICKY-STICKY-THICKY GOO

is ICKY and stICKy

And THICKY!

so it's very hard to move
around in! Are you ready
to give it a go, *ICK*STERS?

Even though I've never crossed a tight-rope before, I don't feel SCARED. Once, my neighbor LoRetta Schmoretta's cat was stuck up in a tree, and I walked across her balcony and clothesline to get him.

I DIDN'T FALL OFF ONCE!

And Peezo is floating on air now that he's done worrying about NICK PUMPERNICKEL so he doesn't care HOW high up we'll be!

BAWK BAAWWK

Oooh, we're about ready to start!

BAGAAAWWWK!

Peezo is so relaxed now that the *Pump-ernator* is out of the picture that he's doing some really **IMPRESSIVE** kicks!

Big G is doing some great kicks too, and Little G is zipping right along, but poor Leeza Schmelly is so afraid of heights that she's clinging to Baa-Baa for dear life!

Way to go, Grandma G!

Hey, Peezo, just a little farther and— **OUCH!** Something just HIT me!

Me too!

LOOK! NICK PUMPERNICKEL is hiding behind that big clump of lumpy bumps! He's using the CHICKPEA SPITTER from another category to try to knock us down!

THIS IS HORRIBLE!

Nick Pumpernickel is being such a SORE LOSER! We won FAIR and SQUARE, and now he doesn't want any of us to win!

OH NO!

Nick Pumpernickel just knocked Little G off the tightrope into the Icky-Sticky-Thicky Goo!

111

I CAN'T BELIEVE IT!

PEEZO IS CHASING NICK PUMPERNICKEL! Big G just told me that when Nick Pumpernickel knocked Little G off the tightrope, Peezo "BUSTED A CRUST" and jumped down and ran after him. OH NO! He's headed right for the *Grump on a Stump*'s yard!

Ha ha, scrawny pizza can't catch the *Pumpernator*!

PEEZO, STOP!

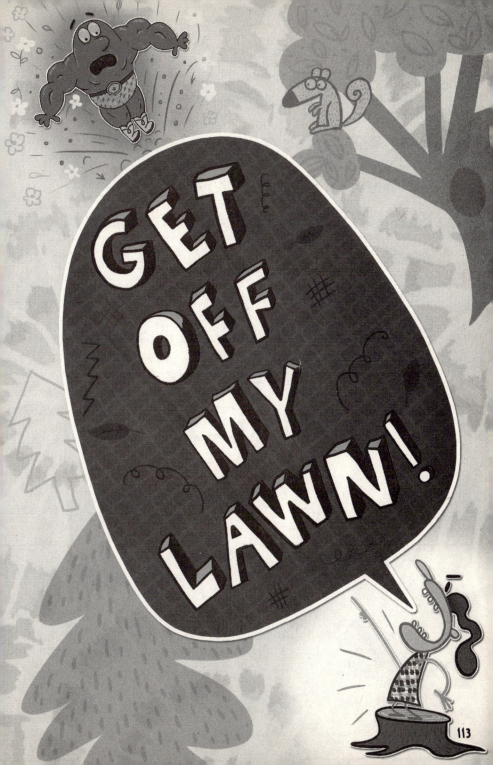

HOLEY DOUGHNUTS!

Peezo stopped himself JUST IN TIME but Nick Pumpernickel wasn't so lucky. He barreled into Maude Ellen Murky's flower beds and trampled her poor petunias! I've never seen her **so mad** and the *Pumpernator* actually looks scared of her! She told him to get busy and clean up the GIANT MESS he made and he's

ACTUALLY

DOING

IT!

AND THAT'S NOT ALL.

Keeping him company is the runaway P. P. Boy himself, Pikyor Pocketo! After he ran off with all the n*ick*els from the *Chopstick Nickel Pick*, he tried taking a shortcut through the *Grump on a Stump*'s backyard.

BIG MISTAKE!

He plowed right through her vegetable garden and ruined her rutabagas!

I must say, it's pretty impressive to see how Maude Ellen Murky is handling it all. She could sure teach the *Law Lads* a thing or two about catching criminals! She even got Pikyor Pocketo to give back the stolen nickels AND Ricky Maverick's wallet, watch, and toupee.

He went THIS way, I bet!

My WIG! I mean, TOUPEE!

GOOD JOB, MAUDE ELLEN MURKY!

CHAPTER 13

LET'S HEAR IT FOR THE LUMPY VALLEY SPINNY ICKY SHOWDOWN DOUBLE CHAMPIONS, THE GRAND GALS AND THE CURLY-CUES! CONGRATULATIONS!

Our name, Grandma!

The SPINNY ICKY SHOWDOWN CHAMPION

The SPINNY ICKY SHOWDOWN CHAMPION

The Grand Gals

Well, if the DOUGH BROS couldn't win THE
SPINNY ICKY SHOWDOWN, I'm glad the *Grand
Gals* did—and the *Curly-Cues* too. After
the combination of

Little G falling off the tightrope,	☹
Big G's fancy kicks,	☺
Leeza Schmelly's fear of heights,	☹
and Baa-Baa's calm, steady pace,	☺

both teams ended up with the **EXACT
SAME SCORE!** As for Peezo
and me—things didn't
really turn out like
we had hoped, but
that's okay.

Mr. Bing always says:

IT'S NOT WHETHER YOU WIN OR LOSE, IT'S HOW YOU PLAY THE GAME.

Or maybe it was:

THE WAY YOU PLAY DOESN'T MATTER BUT WINNING DOES SO DON'T LOSE!

NO, WAIT, I think it was—oh, I don't know.

BUT IT SURE WAS FUN!

AND, an unexpected BONUS of being on the show is that Peezo finally got over his fear of NICK PUMPERNICKEL. It was so brave of Peezo to run after him. And it looks like I'm not the only one who thinks so!

The only **BAD** thing about not winning is that I didn't get the new trophy friend for Stiffy Stu McShiny. I hope he won't be too disappointed.

Here, Arnie. I want you to have this.

Your propeller-spinning-penguin hat? *WHY?*

You could have won the *SPINNY ICKY SHOWDOWN* but you stopped to help me instead. It's my way of saying **THANK YOU.**

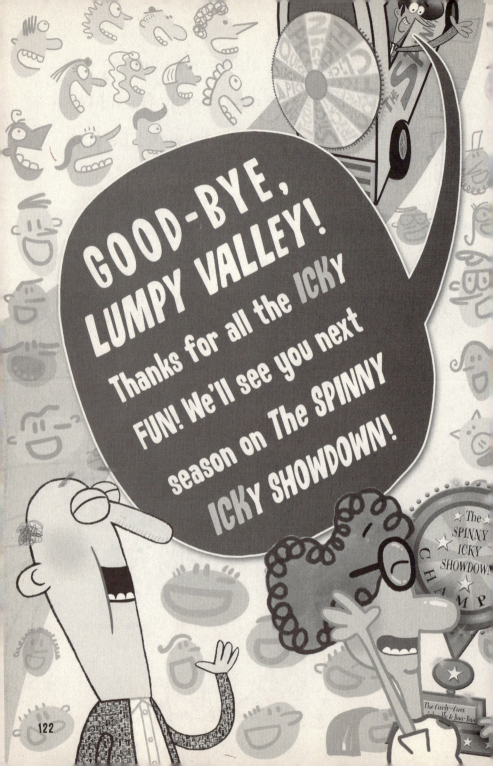